C0-AKI-400

HEAVY WATER

KICKSTART
LOS ANGELES · CALIFORNIA

CREATED BY **JONATHAN W. C. MILLS**

ART & COVER BY **ALBERTO MURIEL**

COLORS BY **VANESA BANOS**

LETTERS & DESIGN BY **BILL TORTOLINI**

EDITED BY **LARRY YOUNG**

PRODUCED BY **KICKSTART COMICS INC.**

For Kickstart Comics Inc:
Samantha Shear, Managing Editor

HEAVY WATER FEBURARY 2011. FIRST PRINTING. Published by Kickstart Comics Inc (480 Washington Ave North, Suite 201, Ketchum, ID. 83340). ©2011 Kickstart Comics, Inc. HEAVY WATER. "HEAVY WATER," the Titles logos, and the likeness of all featured characters are trademarks of Kickstart Comics, Inc. All rights reserved. No portion of this publication may be reproduced or transmitted, in any form or by any means, without the express written permission of Kickstart Comics, Inc.
PRINTED IN USA.

Address correspondence to: Kickstart Comics Inc.
480 Washington Ave., North Suite 201, Ketchum, ID. 83340

NORWAY, 1943
DAWN.

*Translated from Norwegian.

*Translated from Broken Norwegian.

WHUMP

VERY GOOD CITIZEN. STRENGTH IS REQUIRED FOR CITIZENSHIP. POWER IS A COMPONENT OF STRENGTH. THE STATE SALUTES YOUR EFFORT-

BREEP

YOUR SESSION HAS ENDED CITIZEN HAUKELID. WELCOME CITIZEN NETTER. YOUR SESSION BEGINS NOW.

...VERY GOOD. STRENGTH IS REQUIRED FOR CITIZENSHIP. POWER IS A COMPONENT OF STRENGTH. VERY GOOD.

THE NATIONAL
ARCHIVES.

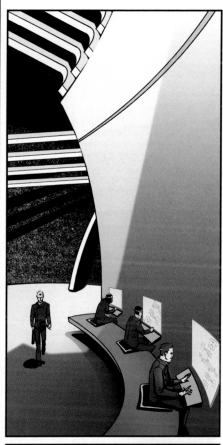

WELCOME
BACK CITIZEN HAUKELID.
PUNCTUALITY NOTED.

TICK

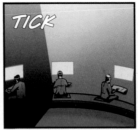

TICK

TICK

HRM.

THE STATE REQUIRES YOUR KNOWLEDGE. DO NOT FORGET TO KNOW YOUR NEIGHBOR.

A GOOD CITIZEN KNOWS HIS NEIGHBOR LIKE HE KNOWS HIMSELF. A GOOD CITIZEN IS USEFUL.

KNOWLEDGE IS STRENGTH. STRENGTH IS REQUIRED FOR CITIZENSHIP...

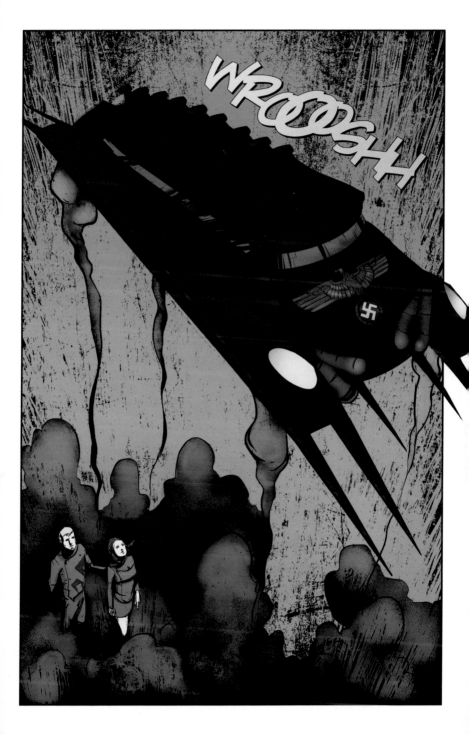

07 30

07 32

07 35

07 35

07 45

08 05

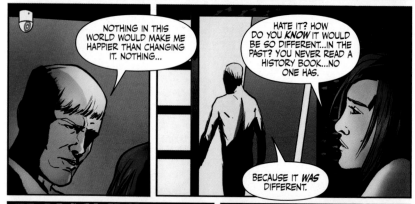

WHERE ARE WE GOING?

YOU'LL SEE, WE ALMOST MISSED IT! IT ONLY COMES TO THE SURFACE ONCE A DAY ON A ROTATING SCHEDULE...

HEY JIMMY.

YOU'RE CLEAN.

THIS IS THE ONLY PLACE IN NEW LONDON WHERE THE HEAT AND ENERGY SIGNATURES CAN BE HIDDEN FROM ABOVE...IT'S TAKEN ALMOST TWO DECADES TO BUILD IT. PIECE BY PIECE.

BUILD WHAT!

IT WAS GIVEN TO ME BY MY FATHER... IT'S A JOURNAL OF A WAR. A BIG WAR. A WAR WITH THE NAZIS... BEFORE THEY CAME TO POWER.

DO YOU KNOW WHAT THIS IS? HOW VALUABLE THIS IS?... HOW DANGEROUS?

YES. I DO.

CAN YOU TELL US MORE? PLEASE...

OKAY...IT WAS WRITTEN GENERATIONS AGO BY A MAN NAMED KNUT HAUKELID. HE WAS A PARTIZAN, LIKE YOU ALL... HE FOUGHT AGAINST THE NAZIS IN NORWAY, A SMALL COUNTRY IN THE FAR NORTH.

HE MOSTLY TALKS ABOUT HARDSHIP AND HOW THEY TRIED TO DESTROY A PLANT THAT THE NAZIS THOUGHT WAS IMPORTANT.

IT WAS A PLANT THAT GENERATED SOMETHING CALLED "HEAVY WATER."

THAT'S AMAZING! HE WAS YOUR RELATIVE!?

THIS IS THE KEY! IF THE NAZIS GET THE WATER...*MIEN GOTT!* THEY ARE THE ONES TO GET NUCLEAR POWER!

IS THAT...?

YES, SHE IS REAL. VERY *VERY* EXPENSIVE.

BEN. WE NEED ACCESS TO THE PAST IN ORDER TO DETERMINE HOW...AND WHEN, WE CAN *CHANGE* IT.

THE ENEMY IS TOO STRONG NOW. WE ARE FIGHTING SOMETHING THAT CAN ONLY BE HARMED IN THE PAST. NOT IN THE NOW.

...AND THIS COULD BE THE KEY. WE ARE FIGHTING A WAR, HERE, BEN. ALL BY OURSELVES, ALL ALONE.

WHAT *IS* THIS? WHAT ARE YOU DOING HERE?

WE ARE FIGHTING TO CHANGE SOMETHING THAT PEOPLE NO LONGER KNOW EVEN HAPPENED...WE ARE FIGHTING A WAR THAT HAS BEEN ERASED BY THE VICTORS.

PIECE BY PIECE.

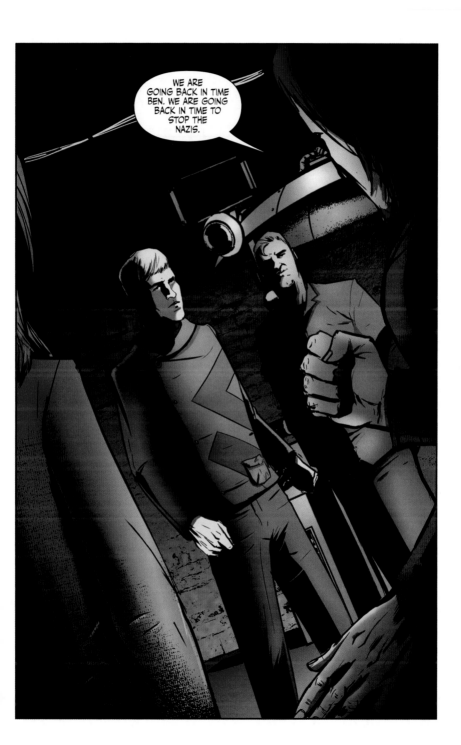

ARE YOU SERIOUS?

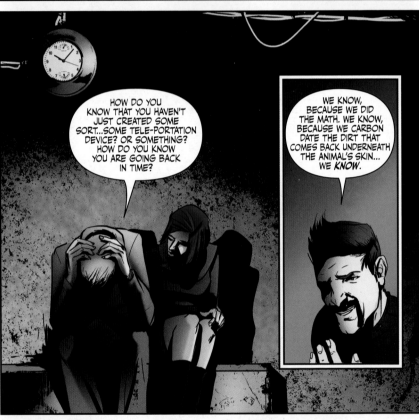

HOW DO YOU KNOW THAT YOU HAVEN'T JUST CREATED SOME SORT...SOME TELE-PORTATION DEVICE? OR SOMETHING? HOW DO YOU KNOW YOU ARE GOING BACK IN TIME?

WE KNOW, BECAUSE WE DID THE MATH. WE KNOW, BECAUSE WE CARBON DATE THE DIRT THAT COMES BACK UNDERNEATH THE ANIMAL'S SKIN... WE *KNOW*.

BEN, CAN YOU READ THIS JOURNAL? *ALL* OF IT?

I'VE READ OR HEARD SOME OF IT EVERY SINGLE DAY OF MY LIFE. MY MOM READ IT, MY DAD... THEY TOLD ME THAT IT WAS IMPORTANT. IT'S A FAMILY HEIRLOOM. OUR DARK PIECE OF FORBIDDEN HISTORY...

BEN, I NEED YOU TO TELL US EVERYTHING. EVERY LITTLE THING. THE NAZIS HAVE DESTROYED ALL THE BOOKS, TAPES, EVERYTHING. YOU KNOW THIS...IT'S ALL BEEN RE-WRITTEN. WE'RE BLIND... LEADING THE BLINDED. WE THOUGHT WE HAD SOMETHING A FEW TIMES... BUT THE LEADS WENT COLD.

HOW LONG HAVE YOU BEEN DOING THIS? DOWN HERE?

TOO LONG, AND THEY'RE STARTING TO SMELL US. THEY KNOW THAT SOMETHING IS HAPPENING.

WE RECRUITED PEOPLE FROM THE EDUCATED CLASS. MYSELF, FLORIA...FINDING PEOPLE LIKE US IS HARD BEN. MOST BELIEVE THE SYSTEM WORKS... THEY THINK NOTHING IS WRONG BUT THE GESTAPO WATCH EVERYTHING...

...THE MACHINE HAS TAKEN *EIGHTEEN YEARS* TO BUILD.

WHY *NOW*? WHY THE PRESSURE?

SINCE JANUARY...

ELAN, LINDA AND GABRIEL HAVE ALL DISAPPEARED. THE ONLY REASON *WE* ARE STILL HERE IS THIS.

CYANIDE. WE ALL HAVE ONE... WE'VE BEEN CHASING A NEEDLE IN THE HAYSTACK OF HISTORY... YOUR JOURNAL COULD BE THAT NEEDLE.

SO, WHY IS MY JOURNAL SO IMPORTANT TO THIS GARTH? I DON'T GET IT.

BECAUSE IT *COULD* POTENTIALLY PROVIDE A TIME AND PLACE TO DESTROY ALL OF THIS BEFORE IT STARTS. THAT'S WHY. THERE ARE VERY FEW RECORDS OF STRATEGIC VICTORIES, BEN.

OKAY... KNUT HAUKELID WAS A FAMILY MAN. HE WAS MARRIED, HE HAD TWO CHILDREN.

BEN, WE NEED TO KNOW ABOUT THE WAR, WHAT DID HE DO?

KNUT HAUKELID LED THE RESISTANCE EFFORTS AGAINST THE NAZIS IN NORWAY.

...ACCORDING TO THE JOURNAL THE NAZIS OBTAINED HEAVY WATER FROM THE VERMOK PLANT. THE ALLIES WERE UNABLE TO STOP IT.

THE WATER WAS IMPORTANT. IT ALLOWED THE NAZIS TO MAKE SOME CRITICAL DISCOVERIES AHEAD OF THE ALLIES...

THE NAZIS TOOK OUR HISTORY AND SMASHED IT. WE KNOW NOTHING. *NOTHING!*

WHAT DOES THE JOURNAL SAY, BEN...WHAT HAPPENED?

THE LAST WORDS ARE: *THEY HAVE THE BOMB. LONDON WAS DESTROYED TODAY...*

I CAN KEEP GOING, IT'S OKA—

SHHHH. I KNOW YOU CAN, BUT MY BROTHER'S NOT THE ONLY PERSON WHO NEEDS YOU DOWN HERE.

YOU DID THE RIGHT THING. YOU KNOW THAT... RIGHT...?

I'M SORRY I TOOK THE JOURNAL. IT WAS TOO VALUABLE TO ASK, BEN.

WE HAVE TO HELP KNUTE STOP THE GERMANS FROM GETTING THE WATER FROM THE PLANT. THAT'S THE FIRST PLACE ULYSSES HAS TO GO. THE PLANT. IF THIS CAN END.

WHAT?

NOTHING. THIS IS OUR WORLD. US TOGETHER. OUR LIFE.

WE HAVE TO HELP THEM.

HALLO, MITT NAV...

YOU NEED TO FIGURE THIS OUT, YOU'VE GOT THREE DAYS...

Tung vann - Heavy Water
Hjelp - Help
Tog - Train
Mitt navn er Ulysses - My name is Ulysses
Jeg er fra fremtiden. - I am from the future.

WHAT DO YOU MEAN?

I MEAN, I AM WORRIED! WE ARE SENDING SOMEONE BACK IN TIME WHO DOESN'T UNDERSTAND THE LANGUAGE, THE CUSTOMS, THE PEOPLE. A STRANGER IN A STRANGE LAND! WE'VE TRAINED HIM ALL WRONG FOR THIS!

HE'S BEEN WORKING WITH US FOR NINE MONTHS...IT'S TOO LATE FOR THIS. HE'S STRONG AND SMART; WE NEED HIM. BEN IS DOING A GOOD JOB.

DON'T YOU GET IT? IF WE CHANGE THE PAST THEN THEY CAN'T GET THE WATER AT ALL. CASE CLOSED!

WHAT IF IT DOESN'T CHANGE IT ENOUGH? WE NEED TO DESTROY THE WATER ITSELF! THEN WE'LL BE SURE THEY DON'T GET IT.

WELL. WE WON'T KNOW EITHER WAY. ONLY ULYSSES WILL KNOW IF IT WAS A SUCCESS.

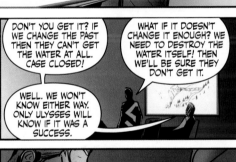

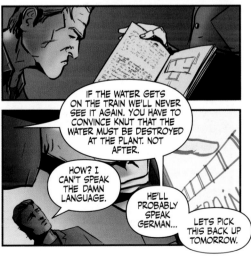

IF THE WATER GETS ON THE TRAIN WE'LL NEVER SEE IT AGAIN. YOU HAVE TO CONVINCE KNUT THAT THE WATER MUST BE DESTROYED AT THE PLANT. NOT AFTER.

HOW? I CAN'T SPEAK THE DAMN LANGUAGE.

HE'LL PROBABLY SPEAK GERMAN...

LETS PICK THIS BACK UP TOMORROW.

BEN, YOU LIVE IN THE PAST ALREADY, IN YOUR HEAD, SO YOU MIGHT AS WELL GO THERE. AND YOU'RE THE ONLY PERSON IN THE WHOLE WORLD THAT WE KNOW WHO CAN SPEAK NORWEGIAN.

OUR MOTHERS, SISTERS, DAUGHTERS AND SONS. WILL ALL CEASE TO EXIST. I...*WE* WON'T EXIST. YOU GET THAT, RIGHT?

DO YOU REMEMBER WHAT I ASKED YOU, IN YOUR APARTMENT? YOU SAID, 'NOTHING WOULD MAKE ME HAPPIER IN THIS WORLD THAN CHANGING IT.'

THIS IS *FOR* US, BEN. FOR *OUR* CHILDREN, FOR *OUR* PARENTS...FOR HISTORY.

WE ARE DESTINED TO BE. THE UNIVERSE MADE US AND SET US ON THE PATH TOWARD EACH OTHER AND TIME HAS *NOTHING* TO DO WITH IT.

NO TIME AND NO TRAINING! THAT'S *SUICIDE!*

I'LL GO. I'LL DO IT.

WE DON'T EVEN KNOW WHO HE IS! WHAT HE'S CAPABLE OF! WE ARE GOING TO TRUST TWENTY YEARS ON HIM? CRAZY!

WE WOULDN'T BE HERE, NOW, WITHOUT BEN. WE WOULD STILL BE SEARCHING AROUND THE DARKNESS OF TIME. BLIND. THERE IS NO ONE BETTER SUITED TO DO THIS THAN BEN. IT MUST BE HIM.

**1943 A.D.
NORWAY**

GERMANY HAS MARCHED RELENTLESSLY
NORTH AND HAS TAKEN COMPLETE CONTROL
OF SCANDINAVIA AND NORTHERN EUROPE.
THE NAZIS ALONG WITH THEIR SPECIAL
BRAND OF CONTROL, DOMINATE THE LANDS
THEY OCCUPY. IN NORWAY A SMALL,
ACTIVE RESISTANCE HAS SPRUNG TO
LIFE AND CONTINUALLY BEDEVILS
THE GERMANS.

...DID ENOUGH OF YOUR MEN SURVIVE TO MAKE THIS A SUCCESS, MAJOR?

I AM GOING TO PERSONALLY ENSURE THAT WE SUCCEED SO THAT THE DEATH OF MY MEN IS WORTH SOMETHING MORE THAN TARGET PRACTICE FOR NAZI BASTARDS...AGREED? WE LOST A CONSIDERABLE AMOUNT OF PLASTIQUE. DO YOU HAVE ANY?

THEY'VE GOT SHARPSHOOTERS HERE...

...AND HERE. THERE'S AT LEAST TWELVE REGULAR ARMY AND TWO SS OFFICERS THAT HAVE BEEN OBSERVED...OVER WHAT? WATER?

IT'S DIDEUTERIUM OXIDE, ALSO KNOWN AS HEAVY WATER. I'M TOLD BY THE EGGHEADS AT MINISTRY IT'S EXTREMELY IMPORTANT FOR THE JERRYS CAPABILITIES. BUT THAT'S ALL I KNOW...

BUT I'M PERSONALLY AWARE THAT THE HIGH COMMAND DIDN'T SEND ME HERE FOR ANYTHING OTHER THAN THE MOST IMPORTANT MISSION OF THE WAR.

THEN WE HAVE TO GO IN HERE, THROUGH THE COOLING SHAFT EXITS...

THIS IS REGULAR ARMY BUSINESS, KNUT. NOT PARTIZAN. WE SHOULD BE TAKING OUT JEEPS ON THE TOLL ROADS. NOT PERFORMING FULL FRONTAL ASSAULTS ON FORTIFIED POSITIONS.

I DON'T WANT MY CHILDREN GROWING UP SPEAKING GERMAN. DO YOU, JONAS?

YOU'RE COMING WITH US. IF YOU COMPROMISE ME OR MY MEN I WILL KILL YOU. THE ONLY REASON I'M NOT DOING SO NOW, IS THAT WE ARE IN THE MIDDLE OF AN OPERATION...

AND YOU HAVE EARNED THE RIGHT FOR ME TO INTERROGATE YOU AFTERWARDS. UNDERSTAND?

HE'S WITH ME.

THERE IS A TRAIN AT THE DEPOT.

THEY WANT TO TAKE THE WATER TO GERMANY, TODAY.

PAFFT

BRAKKA

BRAKKA

YOU DON'T BELIEVE ME. DO YOU?

DOES IT MATTER?

I HAVE A MISSION, YOU NEED TO FOLLOW IT.

EXCEPT *I* KNOW WHAT'S GOING TO HAPPEN! I KNOW THAT WE NEED TO BLOW UP THE WATER ON THE *TRAIN*. NOT THE PLANT.

IF WE DON'T BLOW UP THE TRAIN TODAY, YOU LOSE. *WE* LOSE.

EVEN IF I BELIEVED YOU WE DON'T HAVE TIME.

WE HAVE TO TRY.

THE OTHERS... WE HAVE THIRTY SECONDS BEFORE THIS PLACE BLOWS UP.

THEN RUN...

I DON'T KNOW IF WE GOT IT...

WHA...?

≈HURK≈

HELLO?

IT DIDN'T WORK.

WE FOUND THE PLANT. WE DESTROYED THE PLACE, JUST LIKE WE WERE SUPPOSED TO BUT WE DIDN'T DESTROY THE TRAIN. I THOUGHT WE DID...

IT'S BEEN NEARLY 12 HOURS! WE THOUGHT YOU WERE DEAD.

WHERE'S FLORIA?

SHE THOUGHT YOU WERE GONE BEN. WE ALL DID...

WHERE IS SHE!?

BEN! STOP!

I THOUGHT... GOD, I LOVE YOU.

WHAT HAPPENED?...

THEY FOUND US BEN. THEY ARE AT THE PLAZA...TRYING TO GET DOWN THE SHAFT. WE HAVE BLOWN IT. IT WILL TAKE THEM SOME TIME TO DRILL IT.

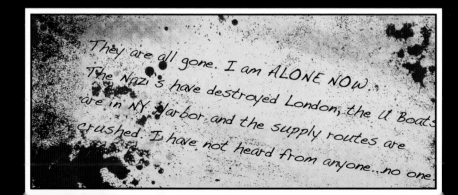

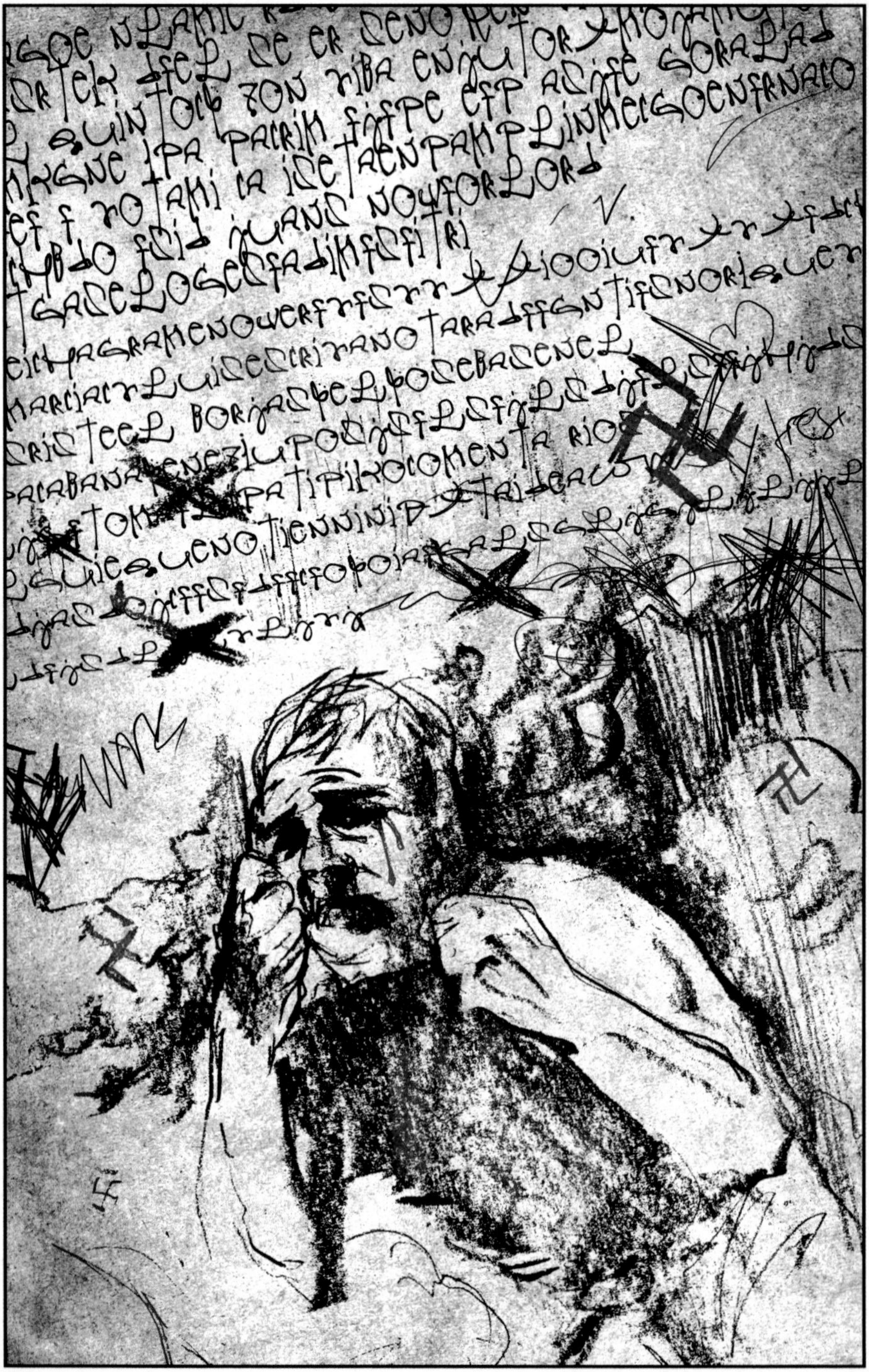

THERE WAS AN AMBUSH. THAT'S WHEN I HAVE TO GO TO GARTH. TWO DAYS AFTER YOU SENT ME BACK LAST TIME.

THEY'VE BREACHED THE TUNNEL...

THE GESTAPO ARE IN THE SHAFT! *THEY'RE COMING NOW!*

YOU CAN'T! BEN, YOU HAVE TO GO BACK. YOUR FIGHT IS THERE. NOT HERE.

FLORIA WAIT!

WHRAMM

WHRAMM

BEN?

HOW MANY ARE YOU?

ALL OF US? HOW DO YOU MEAN?

GET YOUR GUNS OUT. NOW.

WHY?

BECAUSE ACCORDING TO *YOU*... YOU HAVE A FEW MINUTES BEFORE THE GERMANS SPRING A TRAP AND KILL HALF YOUR MEN.

HERE.

USE IT.

CL!CK

YA...
SCHWINE
YA!...
=URK=

HOW DID YOU KNOW!? HOW!? YOU JUST WALK INTO OUR CAMP AND THEN THEY SHOW UP!?

MORE THAN HALF OF YOU WOULD BE DEAD IF THIS MAN HAD NOT TOLD US OF THE GERMANS ATTACK. SO LET IT BE SAID, HERE AND NOW, THAT HE IS ONE OF US.

WHAT IS NEXT?

WE NEED TO DESTROY THE TRAIN. WITH THE WATER ON IT.

THE TRAIN IS GONE. WHEN THE RAID FAILED THEY PACKED IT UP, BROUGHT IN THE REGULAR ARMY AND SENT IT SOUTH YESTERDAY UNDER HEAVY GUARD.

WE SCREWED UP, LEAVING THE SAS GUN BEHIND AT THE PLANT. BY BLAMING IT ON THE BRITISH THE NAZIS KNOW THE WATER'S STRATEGIC. THEY ARE GOING TO DO EVERYTHING IN THEIR POWER TO PROTECT IT AND MAKE SURE WE DON'T SUCCEED TWICE.

THEY ARE TAKING IT TO THE FERRY. WE HAVE TO GET THERE FIRST AND DESTROY IT.

HOW DO YOU KNOW THAT?

BECAUSE YOU ALREADY TRIED IT ONCE...

FAILED...WELL, IT'S A GOOD THING I DON'T KNOW ANYTHING ABOUT THAT.

WE'RE MOVING CAMP, I WANT US OUT OF HERE IN 15 MINUTES.

WHY IS EVERYONE GOING IN DIFFERENT DIRECTIONS?

HARDER TO TRACK US. WE HAVE A RENDEZVOUS.

WE HAVE TO DO THIS ALONE.

WE HAVE TO FIND A DIFFERENT WAY TO GET ONTO THE FERRY AND WE HAVE TO DO IT BY OURSELVES...

WHAT WENT WRONG?

IF WE LEAVE TOMORROW WE CAN GET TO MAEL BY SATURDAY NIGHT...MY COUSIN LIVES THERE. HE WILL SHELTER US.

HOW FAR IS MAEL?

IT'S THREE DAYS OF HARD WALK FROM OUR RENDEZVOUS. WE HAVE TO MOVE. THERE IS NO ROAD IN OR OUT. JUST THE FERRY.

HOW MANY PEOPLE KNOW ABOUT THE RENDEZVOUS POINT?

ALL OF THEM.

KNUT. DO NOT SAY ANYTHING TO ANYONE ABOUT OUR MISSION. IT'S IMPORTANT.

I DON'T TAKE ORDERS FROM YOU. DO NOT FORGET THAT. IF I KEEP SOMETHING FROM MY MEN FOR YOU, IT HAD BETTER BE THE ONLY CALL YOU CAN MAKE. UNDERSTAND?

YOU HAVE A POSSIBLE TRAITOR IN YOUR UNIT. GUNNAR HANSEN

HIS UNIT WAS KILLED! HE WAS THE ONLY SURVIVOR...

BRING HIM WITH US.

THEY HAVE GRETA...MY SONS.

WE *ALL* HAVE FAMILIES...THE MEN THAT ARE DEAD BECAUSE OF YOU HAD FAMILIES TOO.

WE *ALL* MADE CHOICES...

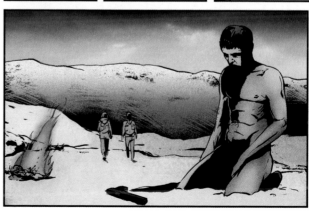

BEN...AM I THE MAN YOU THOUGHT I WAS? FROM THE JOURNAL?

...YES. AND MORE. YOU ARE THE MAN THAT GENERATIONS OF OUR FAMILY HAVE READ ABOUT. A HERO.

I AM NOT DOING THIS TO BE A HERO, BEN. PEOPLE ARE DYING, THIS MATTERS, THIS WAR. THE WHOLE WORLD IS ON A PRECIPICE. IT'S TEETERING I CAN FEEL IT.

THAT'S WHY I'M HERE. TO CHANGE IT, TO HELP YOU PUSH IT BACK FROM THAT BRINK. BECAUSE THIS ONE MOMENT IN TIME, LIKE IT OR NOT, IT MATTERS.

TOMORROW, WE REACH MAEL.

DO YOU HAVE A WIFE? IN THE FUTURE?

I HAD A GIRLFRIEND. FLORIA.

WHY DIDN'T YOU MARRY HER?

I RAN OUT OF TIME.

DON'T WORRY ABOUT ME. BURY THEM. QUICKLY. WE NEED TO MOVE.

THE FERRY WILL ARRIVE TOMORROW MORNING. 10:30AM. IT'S A PASSENGER FERRY, LOTS OF PEOPLE. CIVILIANS. THE NAZIS ARE COUNTING ON US NOT BLOWING UP OUR OWN COUNTRYMEN.

ARE WE?

YOU SAID THERE ARE MILLIONS... BILLIONS OF LIVES AT STAKE ON THIS WATER. RIGHT?

THEN WE BLOW UP THE FERRY. IT WILL TAKE TIME TO SINK, HOPEFULLY MOST WILL MAKE IT INTO THE LIFEBOATS. NORWEGIANS ARE AN ORDERLY SOCIETY...

AREN'T WE DESCENDED FROM VIKINGS?

OLAF...

WE HAVE ONLY ONE CHANCE TO GET ON TOMORROW. OTHERWISE WE MISS THE BOAT ENTIRELY. IT KEEPS GOING...IF IT DOES. WE LOSE.

I HAVE CLOTHES, MY PAPERS CAN GO TO THIS ONE. I DON'T LEAVE MUCH ANYMORE. IT'S FINE.

YOU ARE A GOOD PATRIOT... AND FRIEND.

DON'T LOOK AT THEM, BEN. YOU CAN ONLY HELP THEM BY MAKING THIS WORK. YOUR WORDS.

CAN'T WE TELL THEM TO GET READY? TO SPREAD THE WORD QUIETLY?

WE DON'T KNOW WHO TO TRUST. ANYONE CAN TIP THEM OFF, BE WORKING FOR THEM.

WHEN...?

WE CAN'T BE TOO CLOSE TO THE LAND. IT HAS TO BE THE MIDDLE OF THE LAKE.

IS IT BAD? IN THE FUTURE, WITH THEM IN CONTROL?

IT'S EFFICIENT AND DEADLY. THE GESTAPO ARE RUTHLESS AND THE STATE PURGES THE SICK, THE WEAK, THE EMOTIONAL...WORK IS ALL THAT MATTERS...AND NOTHING IS PRIVATE. NOTHING.

YOUR JOURNAL... IT'S ILLEGAL. OWNING IT, EVEN KNOWING SOMEONE WHO HAD SOMETHING LIKE THAT IN THEIR POSSESSION..

WHY DIDN'T THEY SEND A SOLDIER?

BECAUSE I SPOKE NORWEGIAN. SORT OF.

YOU'RE VERY BRAVE. I HAVE BEEN THINKING. IF THIS WORKS...YOUR FUTURE IT'S...

GONE. YES...YES IT IS.

IT'S TIME.

I KNOW YOU ARE MY FAMILY BENJAMIN HAUKELID. IT MAKES ME VERY PROUD TO KNOW THAT IN SIX GENERATIONS OUR BLOOD HAS NOT THINNED.

GO, MAKE THE FUTURE.

SURVIVE.

EPILOGUE

I WON'T BITE.

WHAT?

I SAID I WON'T BITE. WHAT ARE YOU WORKING ON? IT LOOKS OLD.

IT IS, IT'S A JOURNAL OF MY RELATIVE. FROM WORLD WAR TWO.

COOL. WHAT WAS HE LIKE? IS IT HARD TO READ?

HE WAS STRANGE.... IT'S LIKE HE WENT INTO THE WAR ONE PERSON AND CAME OUT A COMPLETELY DIFFERENT ONE. WAR CHANGES PEOPLE.

MY NAME IS FLORIA.

MY NAME IS BEN. BEN HAUKELID...

NICE TO MEET YOU BEN...HAVE WE MET BEFORE?

THE END

ACKNOWLEDGEMENTS

HEAVY WATER owes many debts towards its creation. The first and foremost is to the bravery of Knut Haukelid and the many brave Norwegians who lost their lives at his side while leading the resistance to the Nazi occupation of their country during WWII.

The time travel concept behind HEAVY WATER has it's genesis in Richard Rhodes 'The History of the Atomic Bomb', a carefully researched history of how human beings came to harness the awesome, dark and unbelievable power of the atom. One of the key conjectures in Rhodes book suggested that had the Nazi's succeeded in transporting the actual heavy water from the Norsk Hydro Plant back to the motherland, their scientists could have fast tracked the development of the bomb for the regime. History is complex and most often written by the victors, but the simple fact remains: without the success Knut Haukelid and his group of partisans we will never know what might have happened...

While some obvious liberties have been taken in the retelling of the story contained in these pages, one thing is true: Knut Haukelid was real. Operations Grouse, Freshman and Gunnerside were real and many soldiers and members of the Norwegian resistance died completing a mission that has continued to resonate through history as one of the most important of the war.

It is the spirit of those soldiers that I have strived to honor in this book. I am humbled and grateful for the opportunity to share my version with a new generation of readers.

Jonathan W.C. Mills

August 2010

Check out these great comics

KICKSTART

WWW.KICKSTARTCOMICS.COM

FOLLOW US ON FACEBOOK AND TWITTER @KICKSTARTCOMICS

apps from Kickstart Comics!

THE BLACKSMITH
MOBILE GAME

Read the comic, play the game!

- Endless gameplay with non-stop action

- Use tilt controls to navigate the streets of New York

- Get chased by hords of enemies

- Build bombs with anything available to push them back

- Unlock exclusive art from the comic book

THE MAKING OF...

FREE APPS for each book featuring behind the scenes images and insight into the story and art

www.KICKSTARTCOMICS.com/APPS

HEAVY☢WATER

KICKSTART

LOS ANGELES · CALIFORNIA